Ever since he was a wee mite (*ter*mite that is), Roberto wanted to be an architect. He longed to follow in the footsteps of such architectural greats as Hank Floyd Mite and Fleas van der Rohe.

Discouraged by comments from family and friends that he is biting off more than he can chew, he decides to follow his dream to the big, buzzing city, where he meets some not-so-creepy crawlers who spark in him the courage to build a community for them all.

Detailed collage illustrations and a witty text bring to life a funny and inspirational story that will encourage readers (and bugs) of all ages to build their dreams.

Praise for *Roberto The Insect Architect*

"Lively. The elaborate, whimsical collages . . . are exceptional. . . . An architectural fantasy picture book for children who dream of building."
—*Booklist*

"Satire-heavy with abundant sight gags and snappy wordplay."
—*Kirkus Reviews*

"Good-natured. . . . Nonstop insect quips and humorous bug house illustrations keep this book buzzing along."
—*Publishers Weekly*

"This charming book combines clever wordplay, exuberant illustrations, and the inevitable message about following your dreams."
—*Architecture*

Winner of the Society of Illustrators Silver Medal
A Smithsonian Notable Book for Children

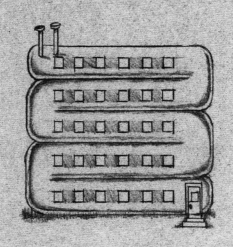

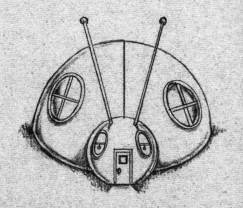

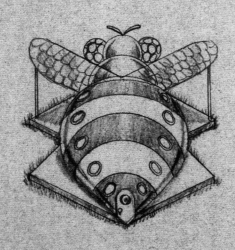

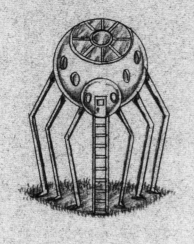

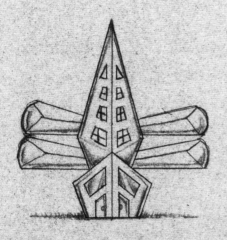

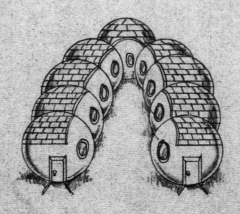

**For my husband, Booth, who shares my passion for old houses,
and for my father, Bob, who wanted to be an architect
once upon a time. — N. L.**

**A special thanks to some friends who helped me work the bugs out:
Victoria Rock and the Chronicle Kids Department, Chauni Haslet, Kim and
Carol in Fremont, Dr. John Beasley, Bill Burbank, and Sarah Boykin.**

First Chronicle Books LLC paperback edition, published in 2016.
Originally published in hardcover in 2000 by Chronicle Books LLC.

ISBN 978-1-4521-5646-0

The Library of Congress has cataloged the original edition as follows:
Laden, Nina.
Roberto : the insect architect / by Nina Laden.
p. cm.
Summary: Roberto the architect, who also happens to be a termite, sets off to the city to find success.

ISBN: 978-0-8118-2465-1
[1. Termites—Fiction.] I. Title.
PZ7.L13735 Ro 2000
[E]—dc21 99-050851 CIP

Manufactured in China.

Design by Catherine Jacobes.
Typeset in Syntax and AdLib.
The illustrations in this book were rendered in mixed-media collage, created with different kinds of paper,
parts of images cut from old catalogs and magazines, wood veneers, cork veneer, blueprints, cardboard,
skeleton leaves, old engravings, stickers, etc., that were glued onto Arches Hot Press Watercolor paper and
painted with Holbein Acryla Gouache. It was all done by hand. No computers were used.

10 9 8 7 6 5 4

Chronicle Books LLC
680 Second Street
San Francisco, California 94107

Chronicle Books—we see things differently.
Become part of our community at www.chroniclekids.com.

ROBERTO
The Insect Architect

Nina Laden

chronicle books · san francisco

Even when Roberto was little, **he went against the grain.** Like most termites, he melted over maple, and pined for pine. Oak was okay, too. But Roberto didn't eat his food. He played with it.

"You're wasting a good meal," his mother said. "Don't you know there are termites starving in Antarctica?" But Roberto didn't answer. He was busy daydreaming about becoming a famous architect.

"Whoever heard of a termite who wanted to be an architect?" the other termites snickered. "Roberto, you should be a chef!" But Roberto didn't want to cook. He wanted to build. **Hungry to start a new life,** Roberto realized he had to leave.

So Roberto packed his bags and took the train to Bug Central Station, in the busy, buzzing hive of the big city. The city was a place where you could **build your dreams.** It was a place where you would be accepted. It was a place where the other termites wouldn't bug you. Roberto beamed hope like a lit-up skyscraper.

But **hope didn't come cheap** in the big city. Neither did a place to live. Roberto had no choice but to rent a room in a flea-bag hotel run by a nervous tick. He shared the room with a family of bed bugs. Roberto introduced himself. Then he built the bed bugs their very own beds.

After a good night's sleep, Roberto began to look for work as an architect. But things didn't go very well.

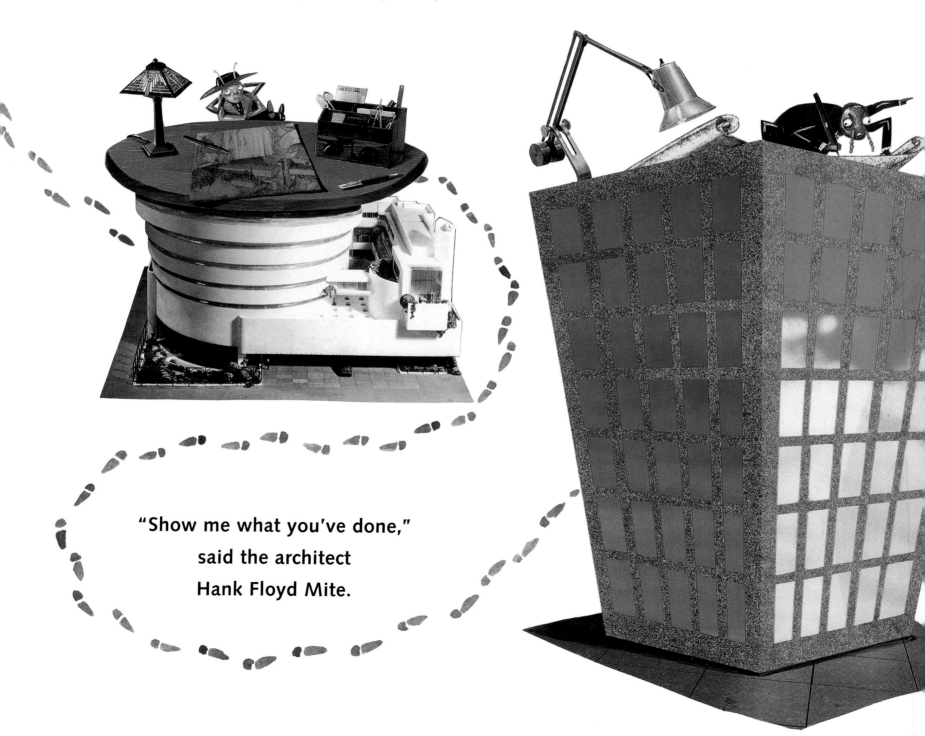

"Show me what you've done,"
said the architect
Hank Floyd Mite.

"There are no termites in my houses,"
stated Fleas Van Der Rohe.

"I'm busy," Antonia Gaudi blurted out.
"Don't BUG me!"

As Roberto crawled home, **feeling like a pest,** he was sideswiped by a fly. "Watch where you're going," he mumbled. The fly started to cry.

"But I don't have any place to go," she lamented.

Roberto wanted to comfort her, but he was nearly nailed by a carpenter ant trying to fix a rickety shed. Then out of nowhere, Roberto was almost run over by a stampede of roaches being chased from a diner. And suddenly, a frantic ladybug flew into his arms.

"My house is on fire and my children are gone!" the ladybug cried.

Roberto could see that he wasn't the only bug with problems. In fact, his problems didn't seem so big after all. Roberto wished he could do something for the others, but what could one termite do? "A lot of damage," Fleas Van Der Rohe had told him.

"I'll show Ol' Fleas what this termite can do. **I'll show them all,**" said Roberto.

Back at the hotel, Roberto
came up with a plan. First, he
drew up some blueprints. He sketched houses
and streets. He sketched stores and playgrounds.
By the time he was finished, he had sketched an entire
neighborhood. "Now I just need to find a good location,"
he declared.

Roberto searched all over the city for the perfect site.
He finally found an abandoned, run-down block of
crumbling buildings. It was a total mess. There were
piles of old wood and garbage everywhere. **It was
just what he was looking for.**

Roberto hammered and nailed.

He sawed and sanded.

He worked day and night.

Like a magician, he transformed the block of junk into a street of extraordinary homes. Each one was **a work of art.** But Roberto didn't sign his artwork. Instead he anonymously sent the keys to the new owners. Then he rolled up his plans and went home.

Some very surprised bugs went home, too. Tudor, the fly with no place to go, buzzed with delight.

"I am a house fly again," she declared.

Then Grant, the carpenter ant, arrived. He dropped his tool belt on the porch.

"Now I can have a real workshop," he beamed.

The roaches were the next ones on the scene.

"You won't find us sleeping in salads anymore," they rejoiced.

Finally, Dotty, the ladybug, and her children moved into their new lair.

"It's perfect," she sighed. "It's fireproof!"

Quickly, word spread. Soon everyone wanted to know who built these amazing abodes. Rumors were flying. **Antennae were buzzing.**

Barbara Waterbugs wanted an exclusive interview.

Robin Leech promised to make the builder rich and famous.

Steven Shieldbug
wanted the movie rights.

Diane Spider searched the
World Wide Web for the scoop.

And **The Insect Inquirer** offered a reward
to the first bug who brought the builder to light.

All day long, bounty-hunting butterflies took wing.
Paper wasps swarmed the streets. Bold weevils
crawled out of the woodwork. But late at night,
a click beetle got the shot.

The next morning,
headlines screamed the news.

INSECT INQUIRER

"TERMITE CHIPS NEW HOMES
OUT OF OLD BLOCKS!"

"It's Roberto," Tudor hummed.

He's our HERO!

Overnight, Roberto became **the talk of the town.**
Architects offered him jobs. Book publishers
wanted his story. Ladybugs sent him love
letters. And his bug buddies threw him
a big bash. At the height of the party,
the Mayor unveiled a statue of
Roberto to be placed in
the city park.

ROBERTO
INSECT ARCHITECT

WINGFLY MUSEUM

Roberto built his dream. He opened his own company and became the most famous architect in the insect world. Students studied him in school. Some of his houses even became museums.

But best of all, when little termites play with their food,
now their parents say:

"Be creative!

Maybe someday you'll grow up
to be just like Roberto."

EXTRA!
ROBERTO BUILDS
FIRST HOUSE ON MARS

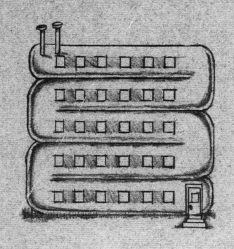

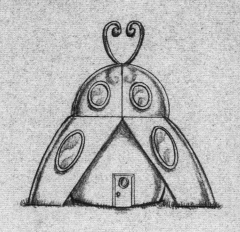

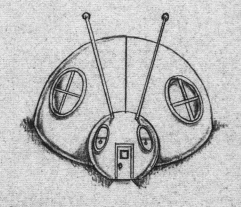
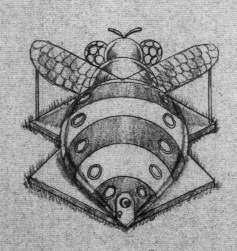

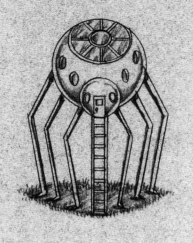

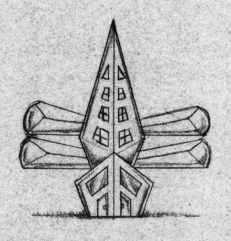
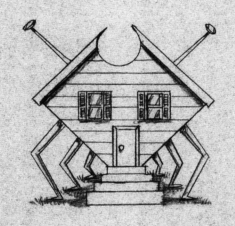

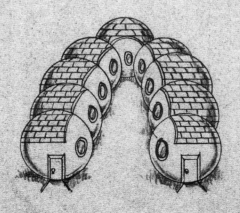

Nina Laden is the author and illustrator of many books for children, including *Peek-a Who?*, one of Scholastic *Parent & Child* Magazine's 100 Greatest Books for Kids; its companions *Peek-a Zoo!*, *Peek-a Boo!*, and *Peek-a Choo-Choo!*; *The Night I Followed the Dog*; *When Pigasso Met Mootisse*; *Are We There Yet?*; and *Once Upon a Memory*, illustrated by Renata Liwska. She lives in Seattle and Lummi Island, Washington.